ANIMALS IN DANGER

LIONS

By Emily Kington

Words that appear in **BOLD** are explained in the glossary.

First published by Hungry Tomato Ltd in 2022
F1, Old Bakery Studios, Blewetts wharf,
Malpas Road, Truro, Cornwall, TR1 1QH, UK.

www.hungrytomato.com

ISBN 978-1-914087-58-5

A CIP catalog record for this book is available from the British Library.

Manufactured in the USA.

Picture credits
(t=top, b=bottom, m=middle, l-left, r=right, bg= background)

Alamy: 4-5bg. **Corbis:** 8-9bg, 16-17bg, 25ml, 25tr, 25bl, 26tr, 26b, 27bl. **Shutterstock**: Alta Oosthuizen 13mr; Ana gram 14-15bg; Bhasmand Mehta 19br; Dagmara Ksandrova 6-7bg; Danita Delimont 25br; Erika J Mitchell 30br; Fumanyc 22-23bg; Hilton 20-21bg, 24bl; Imageportal 29bl; Kakuli 12-13bg; Kirill Dorofeev 31bg; Kovop58 29ml; Maggy Meyer 1bg,10tl, 27t; Mees Kuiper 9br; Milan Zygmunt 10-11bg; NathanAN 15br; Ondrej Prosicky 3bg, 30tr; PinkeshTanna 18-19bg; Rudi Hulshof 23br; RujStudio 2bg; Silvia Truessel 28br, 32br; SteffenTravel mr, 28m; Thomas Retterath 29 tr; WOLF AVNI 5br, 24ml.

Every effort has been made to trace the copyright holders, and we apologize in advance for any unintentional omissions. We would be pleased to insert the appropriate acknowledgements in any subsequent edition of this publication.

CONTENTS

THE GRASSLANDS OF AFRICA

Life isn't easy for animals on the grasslands of Africa.

At some times of year, there is heavy rain. At other times it is as dry as in a desert.

Huge numbers of animals live on the grasslands. Antelopes and zebras eat the tough grass. Giraffes feed on the thorny trees.

Many **predators** live in this **habitat**, such as cheetahs, leopards, and the largest grassland predator – the lion.

DID YOU KNOW?

The size of the pride depends on how much food and water there is available.

THE PRIDE

A family of lions is called a pride.

The pride may have many females, called lionesses, but only between one and four males.

When young male lions are two to four years old they will leave their pride. Sometimes they will stay together in male groups.

When they are old enough, male lions look for a pride of their own to take over.

MALE LIONS

Male lions are larger than females, and their manes make them look even bigger.

Adult male lions are in charge of the pride. They guard the pride's **territory** and keep the group safe.

Males leave their scent on trees and rocks, and roar loudly to warn other lions to stay away.

A male lion will lead his pride until a younger and fitter male fights him and takes over.

DID YOU KNOW?

All lions have black hairs at the end of their tails.

Lionesses will have two to four cubs at one time. They give birth in a den, hidden away in rocks or long grass.

Cubs feed on their mom's milk until they are six months old. When they are about six weeks old they will start to eat some meat caught by their mom.

The females in a pride share the job of looking after the cubs.

DID YOU KNOW?

Lionesses carry their cubs in their mouths.

LION CUBS

HUNTING FOR FOOD

Lions will hunt at any time, but they prefer to hunt at night.

Lionesses do most of the hunting. Male lions are big and heavy, and not as fast as the females.

Lions get some of their food by **scavenging**. They look for animals that have died, or have been killed by another predator.

DID YOU KNOW?

Lions can see in the dark six times better than a human.

Lioness moving through tall grass to sneak up on her prey.

MAKING WAY FOR PEOPLE

Life is becoming tougher for the lions of Africa. They are having to make way for humans.

Some of these people are miners looking for **minerals** and metals in the ground.

When the miners find valuable minerals, large areas of grassland can be destroyed or **polluted**.

Local lions may be seen as a danger to workers and shot.

Mining construction workers on a mountaintop in Sierra Leone, Africa.

In the African countries where lions live, human populations are growing.

Towns are spreading, and more and more of the grasslands are becoming farmland.

Without the grasslands, **prey animals**, such as zebras and antelopes, will disappear. Hungry lions will attack farm animals if they have no prey to hunt.

Many lions are shot by farmers who do not want lions killing their cattle.

LIONS AND FARMERS

DID YOU KNOW?

Hunting lions for sport is allowed in some places in Africa. Hunters kill the animals, so that they can have a dead lion as a trophy.

ASIATIC LION

If the African lions are not helped they could be in as much danger as their cousins, the Asiatic lions.

DID YOU KNOW?

Asiatic lions are smaller than African lions, and the males have smaller manes.

Around 200 years ago, the Asiatic lion was found from India all the way to Europe.

Now, because of hunting and habitat destruction, there are fewer than 600 Asiatic lions left in the world.

The only place they live wild is in the Gir National Park in India.

A wild Asiatic female lion marking her territory in Gir National Park, India.

A SAFE HOME

The best way to make sure that lions have a future is to find them a safe place to live.

In Africa, some countries have set up **wildlife reserves**. It is against the law to hunt animals in the reserves.

Wardens protect the animals and make sure that there is enough grassland to feed prey animals, such as antelopes and zebras.

Lions can be brought into the reserves from places where they are not safe.

Group of lions drinking in Sabi Sands Game Reserve, Greater Kruger, South Africa.

DO LIONS HAVE A FUTURE?

The future of the lions depends on people.

It might seem a bad idea to bring **tourists** into the wildlife reserves to look at lions, but the lions soon get used to visitors.

Wildlife tourists spend money, which helps make jobs for the people who live in or near the reserves. This means that protecting the lions and other wild animals is important to local people.

Farmers who live in the area also understand that they must share the reserve with the lions.

FACT FILE

THE WORLD OF THE AFRICAN LION

African lions live on grasslands in the red areas on the map.

• Lions are doing well if they live in wildlife reserves. But in other areas, lions are disappearing fast.

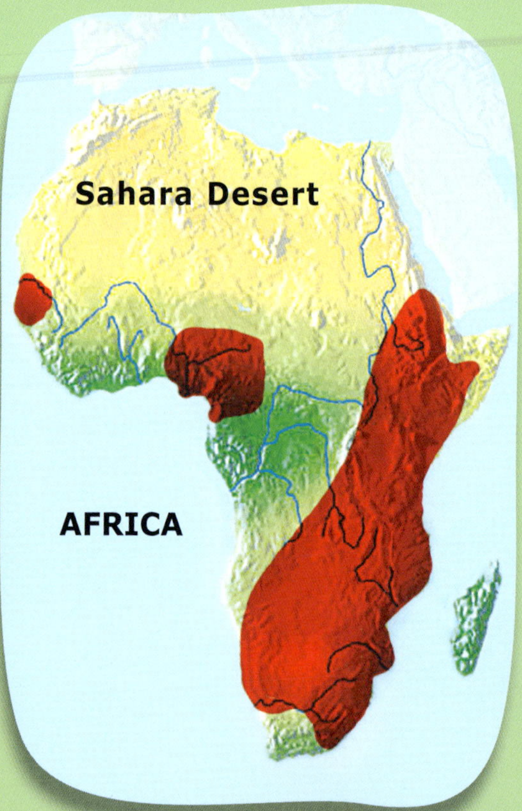

ANIMALS OF THE GRASSLANDS

Predators:

Lions, leopards, cheetahs and hyenas.

Prey animals:

Buffaloes, wildebeests, antelopes, giraffes, zebras and warthogs.

LION BODIES

Here are some facts about lion bodies:

- A male lion has a mane to make him look big and scary to other males.
- The mane also protects the lion when he fights.

- A cub's coat has spots and stripes, which fade away when they are about 3 months old.

Male
Length: up to 10 ft
(including tail)
Weight: up to 530 lbs

Female
Length: up to 8.2 ft
(including tail)
Weight: up to 400 lbs

FACT FILE

LIONS IN DANGER

There are many problems facing lions today:

- **Climate change** is an increasing threat to lions. Rising temperatures and droughts lead to less water for both lions and their prey.

- The lions' habitat is disappearing as people need more land to live, mine and farm.

- This lack of habitat brings lions closer to people and their livestock than ever before. Some people will shoot lions to try to protect themselves and their animals.

- Lion bones are sometimes used in Chinese medicine, and they are still being hunted illegally for them.

FACT FILE

CONSERVATION

Conservation groups are working hard to help save wild lions.

- Wildlife reserves have been set up to protect lion habitats. They also need to protect the lions' prey animals to make sure they have enough to eat.

- Wildlife reserves provide jobs and money for local people, which makes them want to keep looking after the wild animals and their habitats.

* Wildlife tourism helps to bring money to the reserves, but it must be done carefully so the animals are not disturbed.

* Some big cats, including lions, are kept in poorly run zoos and circuses. Conservation groups try to rescue these animals and find them safe new homes.

HOW YOU CAN HELP

There are some great animal conservation charities and wildlife reserves that need money to pay for the work that they do. There are lots of fun ways that you could help to raise money and awareness for them.

- Why not organize a tasty bake sale?
- Ask people to sponsor you to do an activity. This could be something like a walk or a run, or helping to pick up trash in your local area.
- Put on a community or school event. How about a disco or a charity run?

Don't forget to get your family, friends and teachers involved! It'll be easier and much more fun with some help!

GLOSSARY

conservation Taking care of the natural world.

climate change Rising global temperatures and changing weather patterns caused by a build up of gases in Earth's atmosphere.

den An animal's home, or a hidden place where an animal sleeps or has its babies.

grasslands Dry areas covered with grass where only a few bushes and trees grow.

habitat A place in the wild that suits a particular animal or plant.

manes The long hair around the necks of male lions.

minerals Valuable substances, such as gold or platinum, found in the earth.

polluted Damaged by trash, or by chemicals and oils that have escaped onto land, water, or into the air.

populations The number of people or animals that live in particular places or countries.

predators Animals that live by killing and eating other animals.

prey animals Animals that are hunted by other animals for food.

scavenging Looking for meat that other predators have left, or from animals that are already dead.

territory The area in which an animal or a family of animals lives.

tourists People who are visiting on vacation.

wardens People whose job it is to look after protected reserves and the animals that live there.

wildlife reserves Places set aside for wild animals and plants to live. The animals and their habitat are protected by laws.

INDEX